WITH ORIGINAL ILLUSTRATIONS
BY GARTH WILLIAMS FROM ALL

LITTLE
HOUSE
COLORING BOOK

Laura Ingalls Wilder

HARPER
An Imprint of HarperCollinsPublishers

This book is set in Stempel Schneidler Medium, designed by F. H. Ernst Schneidler,
and Little House Script, a typeface based on Laura Ingalls Wilder's
handwritten correspondence, by Julia Sysmäläinen.

HarperCollins®, Little House®, and The Laura Years™ are trademarks of HarperCollins Publishers Inc.

Little House Coloring Book
Copyright © 2016 by Little House Heritage Trust

www.littlehousebooks.com

ISBN 978-0-06-257231-8

Typography by Jenna Stempel

23 24 25 PC/BRR 10 9 8 7

❖

First Edition

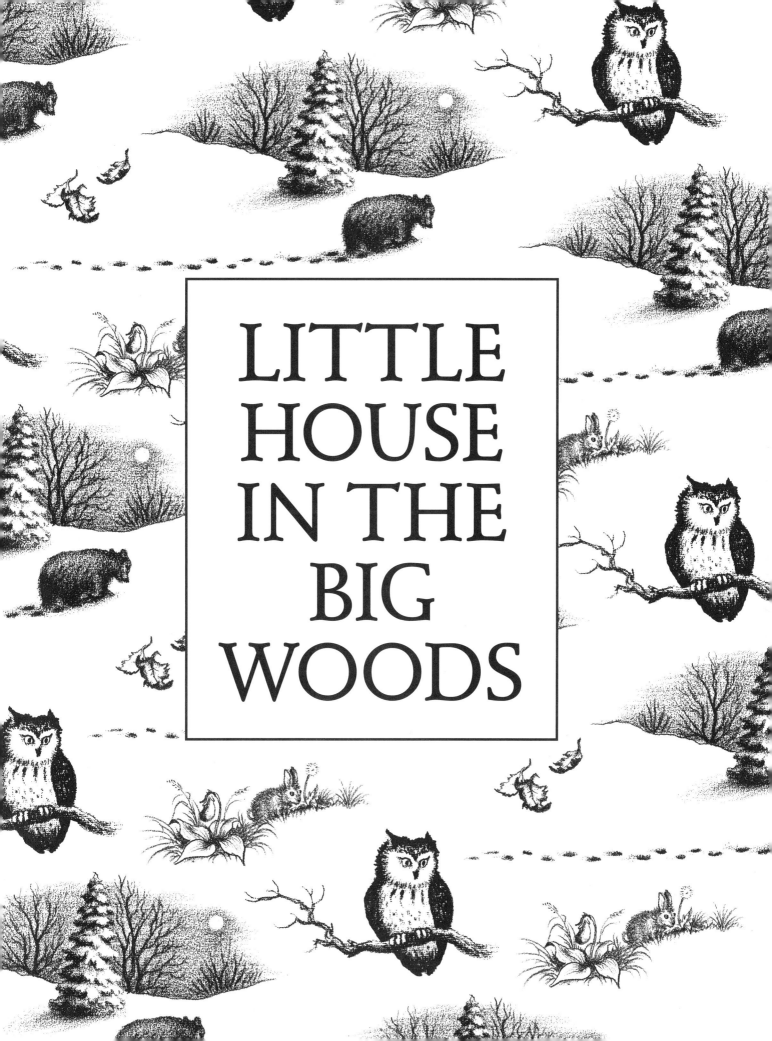

LITTLE
HOUSE
IN THE
BIG
WOODS

Once upon a time, sixty years ago, a little girl lived in the BIG WOODS of Wisconsin, in a little gray house MADE OF LOGS.

He was blowing up
THE BLADDER.
IT MADE A LITTLE
white balloon,
and he tied the end
TIGHT
with a string.

Laura had only a CORNCOB wrapped in a HANDKERCHIEF, BUT IT WAS *a good doll.*

"THEN JUST AS THE SLED
WAS SWOOPING
TOWARD THE HOUSE,
A BIG BLACK PIG
STEPPED OUT OF THE
WOODS."

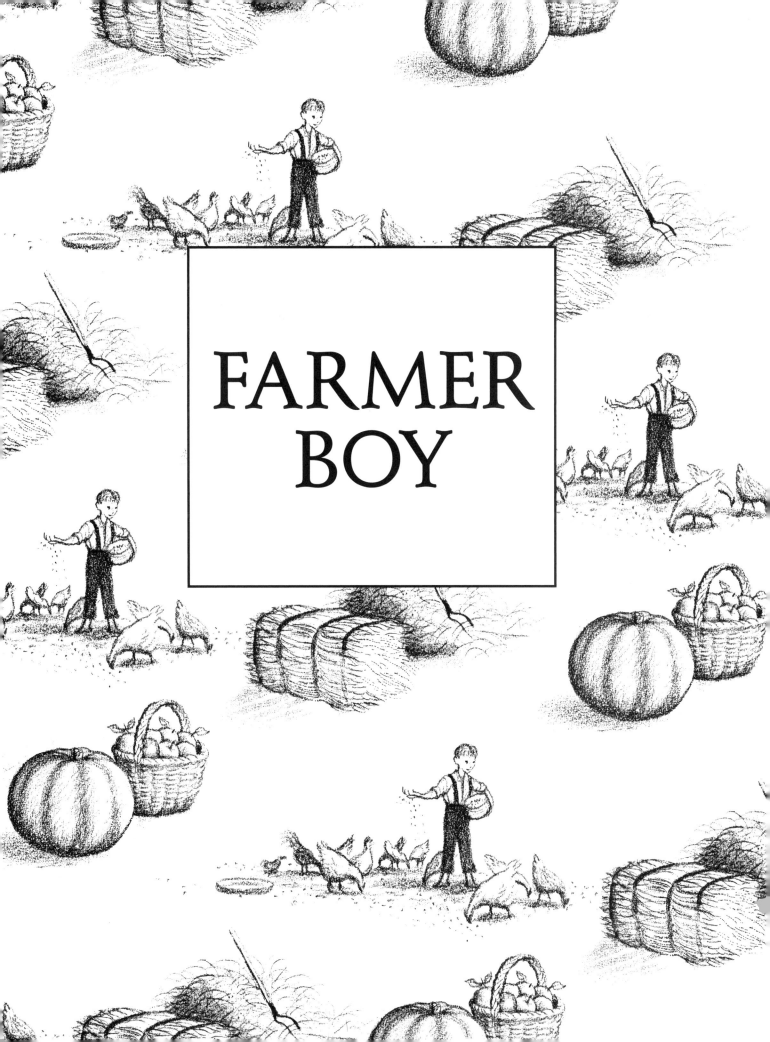

FARMER
BOY

DOWN A
LONG ROAD
through the woods
a little boy
TRUDGED TO SCHOOL,
with his big brother Royal
and his two sisters,
Eliza Jane
AND Alice.

THEY ALL
SETTLED DOWN
cosily by the
BIG STOVE
in the
dining-room wall.

The fifes
TOOTED
and the flutes
SHRILLED

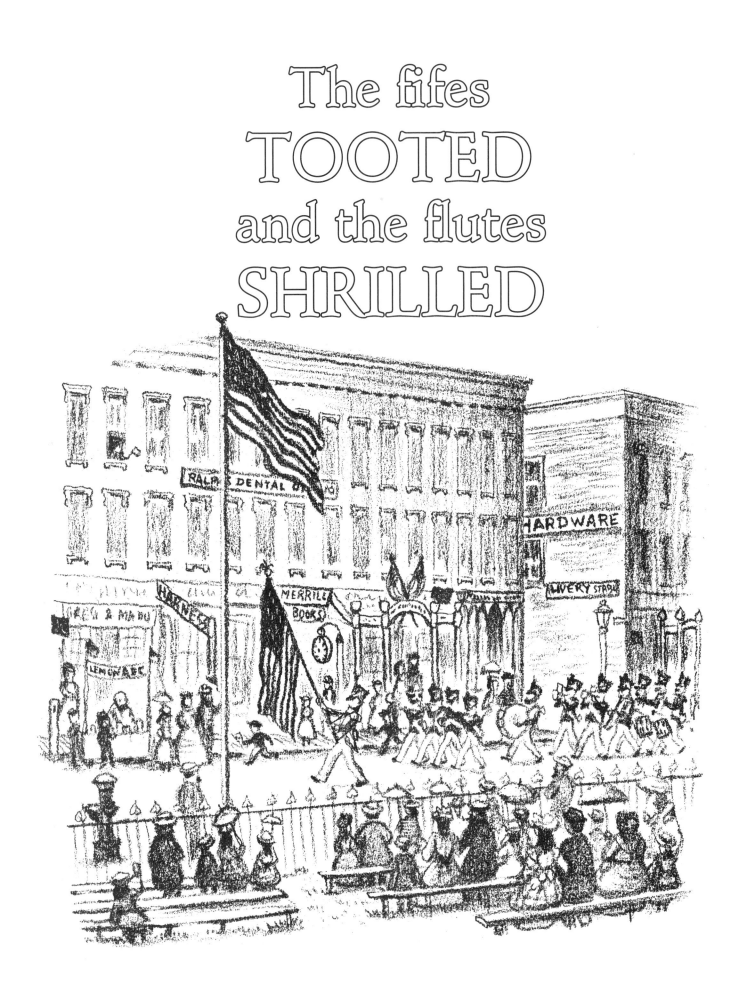

and the
DRUMS
came in with
RUB-A-DUB-DUB.

Almanzo STARED, and the bear STARED BACK at him with *little, scared eyes* above his MOTIONLESS PAWS.

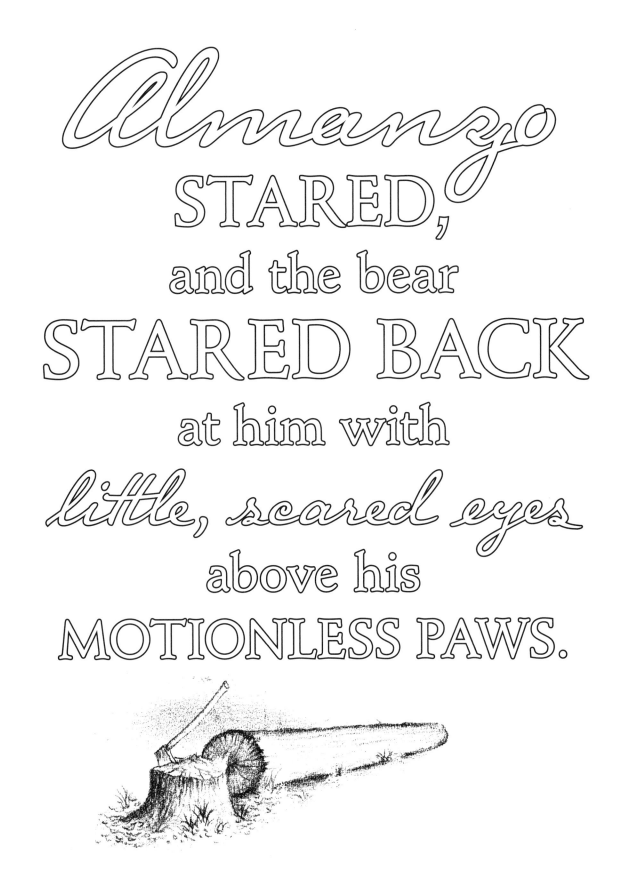

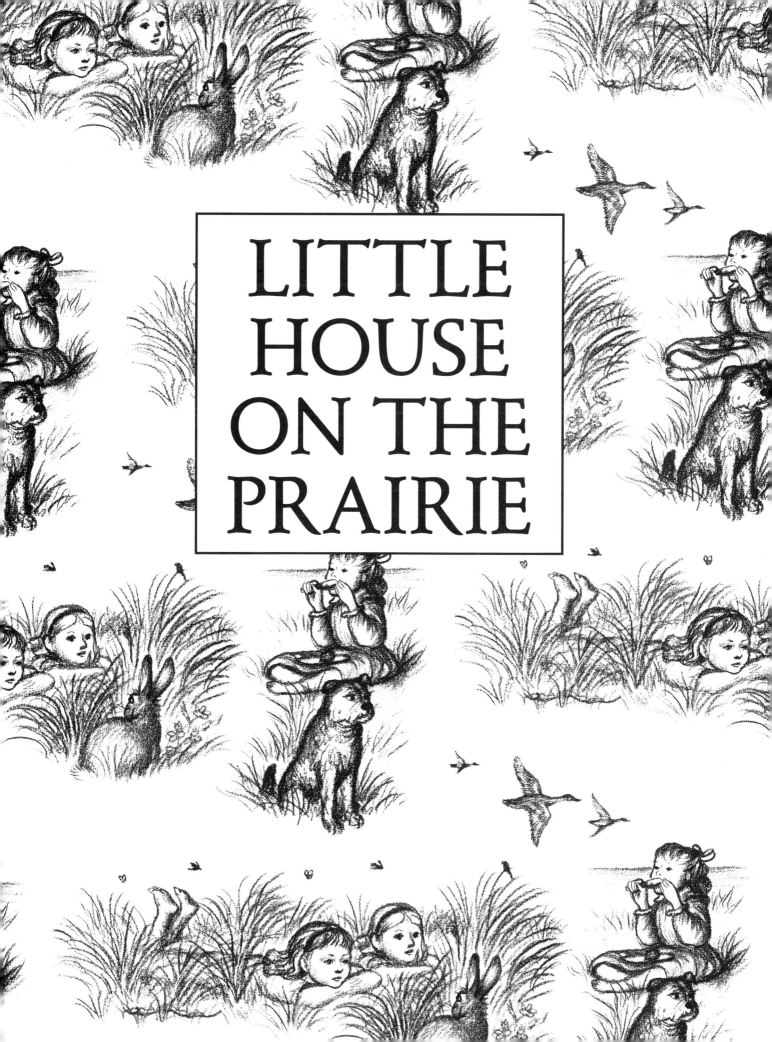

LITTLE HOUSE ON THE PRAIRIE

A LONG TIME AGO,

when all the grandfathers and
grandmothers of today were
little boys and little girls
or very small babies,
or perhaps not even born,

PA and MA and
MARY and LAURA and
BABY CARRIE
left their LITTLE HOUSE in the
Big Woods
of WISCONSIN.

Mary sat
PERFECTLY STILL
beside a hole,
WAITING FOR ONE
to come up, and

JUST BEYOND *her reach* gophers scampered MERRILY.

Pa had taken the CANVAS WAGON-TOP off the house, and now he was ready TO PUT THE ROOF ON.

Perhaps Mary felt *sweet* and good inside, but LAURA DIDN'T. When she looked at Mary SHE WANTED TO SLAP HER. So she dared not look at MARY *again.*

"JACK'S not afraid of *anything,* EVER!"

You never know what will happen next, nor where you'll be TOMORROW,

when you are *traveling in a* COVERED WAGON.

ON THE BANKS OF PLUM CREEK

The path went across short sunny grass, to the edge of *the bank.*

Down below it was the creek, rippling and glistening in the *sunshine.*

ITS EYES SPARKLED MAD, AND
FIERCE WHITE TEETH
SNAPPED ALMOST
ON LAURA'S NOSE.

"I'M FLYING!
I'm flying!" she sang.
Mary climbed up,
and Mary
BEGAN TO FLY, TOO.

RED and BLUE and  PURPLE and ROSY-PINK and WHITE and STRIPED  flowers all had their throats WIDE OPEN as if they were singing glory to the morning.

"YOU keep your hands off my doll, LAURA INGALLS!"

BY THE SHORES OF SILVER LAKE

Laura was *washing the dishes* one morning when OLD JACK, lying in the sunshine on the doorstep, GROWLED to tell her that SOMEONE WAS COMING.

THE VELVET SEAT
was springy.
Laura wanted to
BOUNCE
on it, but she must
behave properly.

She AND THE *pony* were going **TOO FAST** but they were going *like music*

and nothing
could happen to her
until the music
STOPPED.

A long, wild, wolf

HOWL

rose and faded away
on the stillness.

ANOTHER

ANSWERED IT. THEN

silence again.

And, as she fell asleep
still thinking of
VIOLETS and
FAIRY RINGS and
MOONLIGHT
over the
WIDE, WIDE
LAND,

where their
VERY OWN
homestead lay,
PA AND THE FIDDLE
were softly
singing.

THE
LONG
WINTER

THE MOWING MACHINE'S *whirring sounded cheerfully* from the old buffalo wallow south of the claim shanty, WHERE BLUESTEM GRASS *stood thick and tall* and Pa was cutting it for hay.

ON THE

HIGH TOP

OF THAT LOAD,

UP AGAINST THE

BLINDING SKY,

A BOY WAS

LYING.

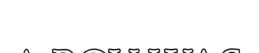

He was *making pancakes,* not because Royal COULD BOSS HIM any more but because Royal could not make GOOD PANCAKES.

Laura's STICK OF HAY WAS uneven and raggedy, not smooth and hard LIKE PA'S.

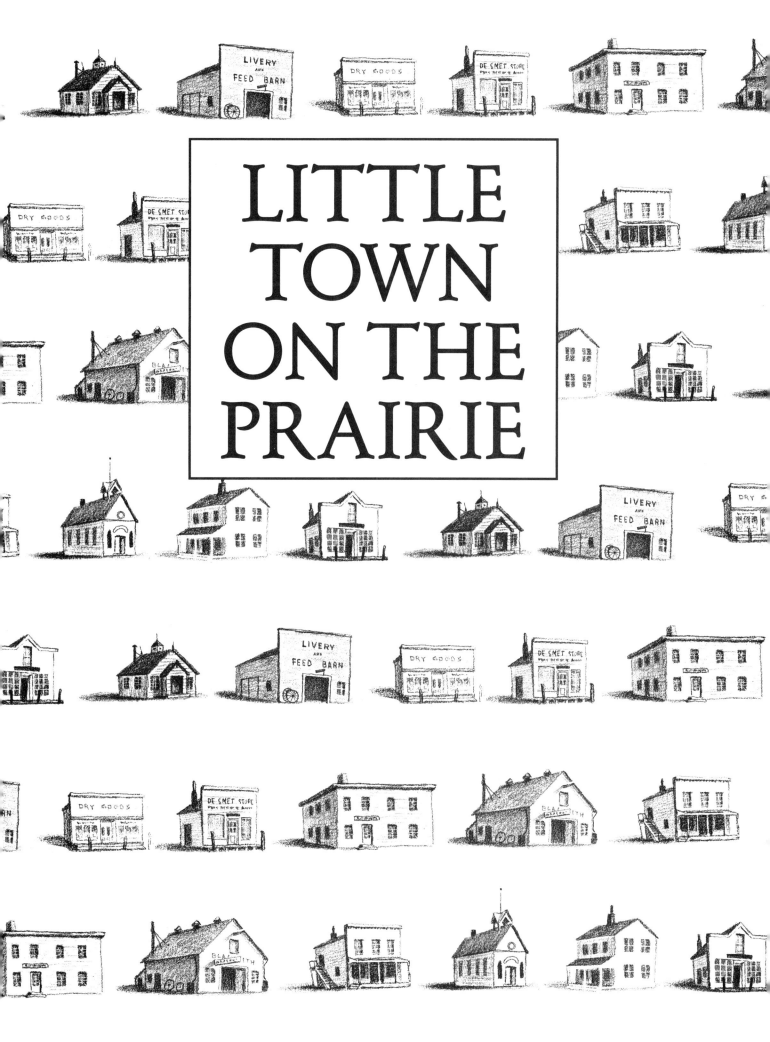

LITTLE
TOWN
ON THE
PRAIRIE

One evening
at supper, Pa asked,
"How would you like to
WORK
IN TOWN,
LAURA?"

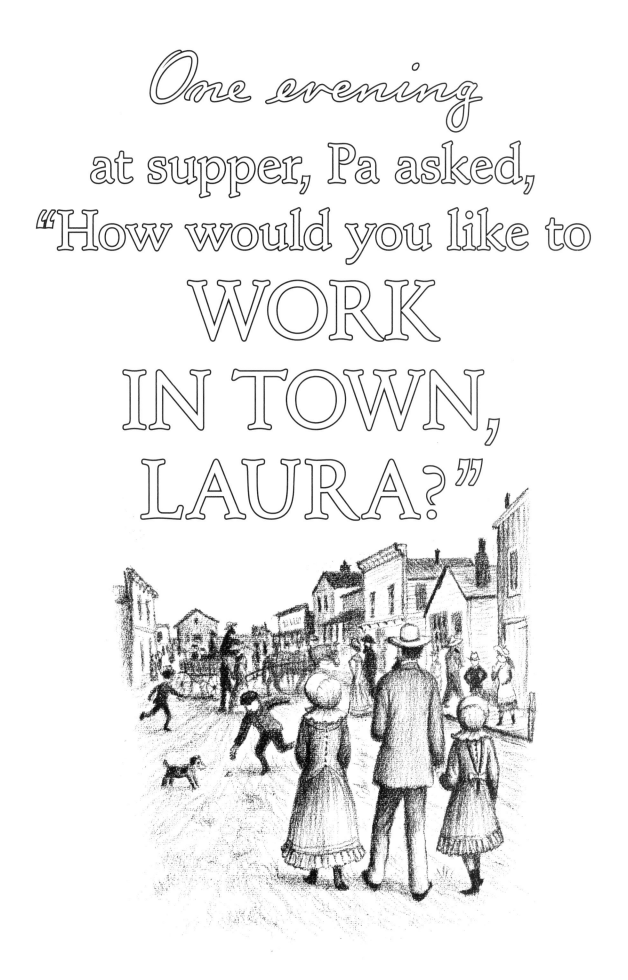

Laura
must keep it from
SPILLING THE MILK,
if she could, and
she had to teach it
HOW TO DRINK,
because it didn't know.

"A KITTEN,"
she said
wonderingly.
"Such a very
LITTLE KITTEN."

Laura was on her feet. HER FURY took possession of her, she did not try to resist it, she gave way completely.

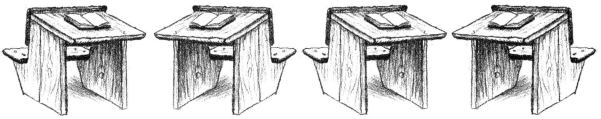

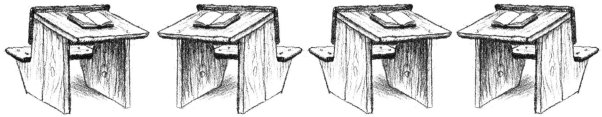

THESE
HAPPY
GOLDEN
YEARS

Sunday afternoon was clear, and the SNOW-COVERED *prairie* sparkled in the SUNSHINE.

"That is the
TEACHER'S TABLE,"
Laura thought,
and then,
"OH MY;
I am the
TEACHER."

"It's like flying!"
Laura said. She had
never
IMAGINED
such wonderful speed.

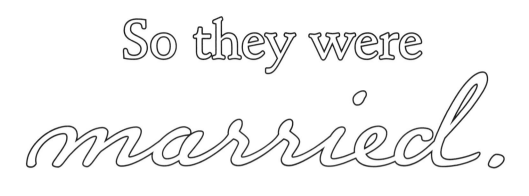

So they were *married.*

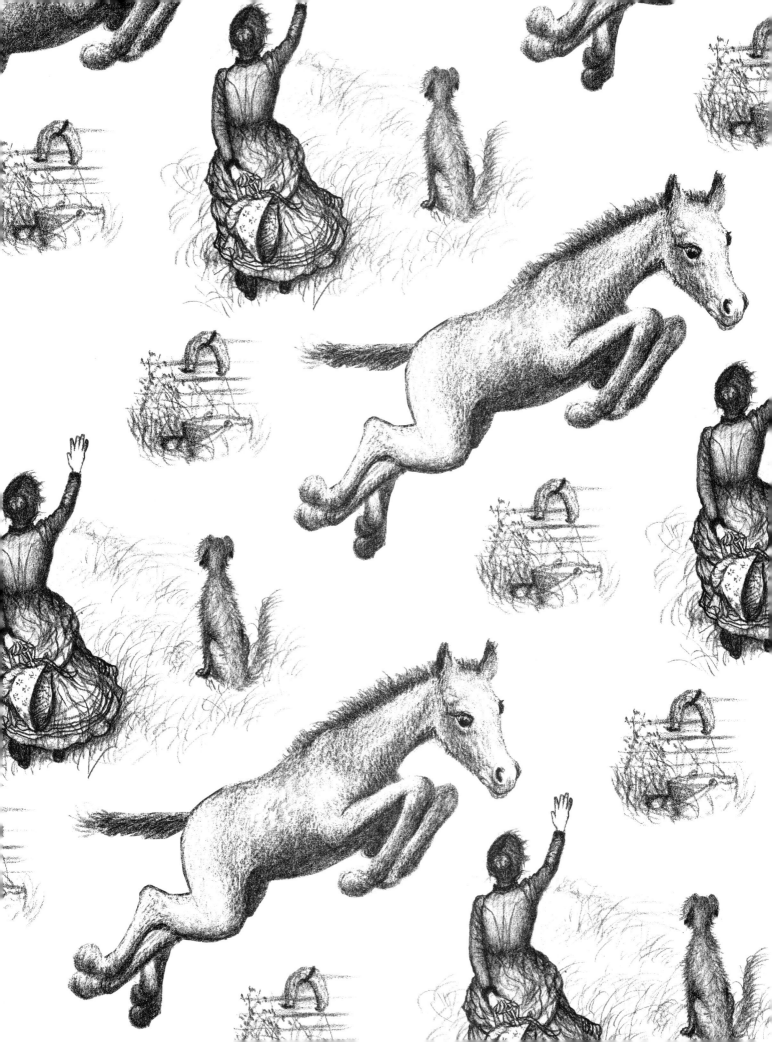

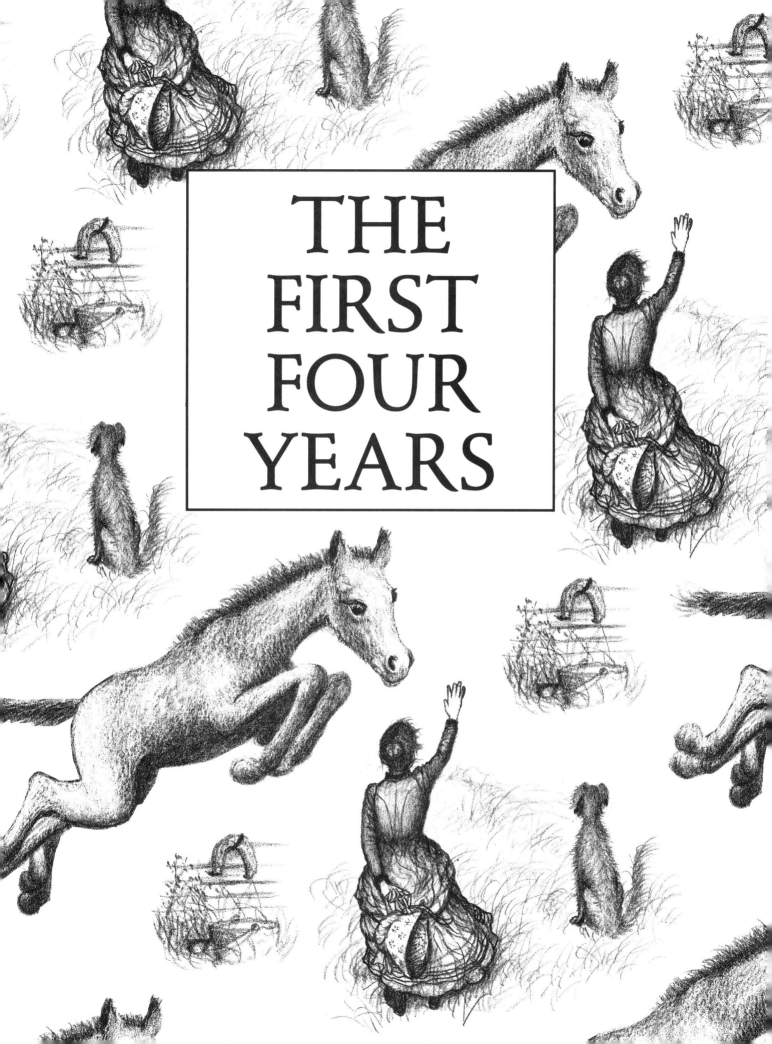

THE
FIRST
FOUR
YEARS

The
stars hung
LUMINOUS and LOW
over the
PRAIRIE.

Rose

spent her time

PLAYING

in the yard now.

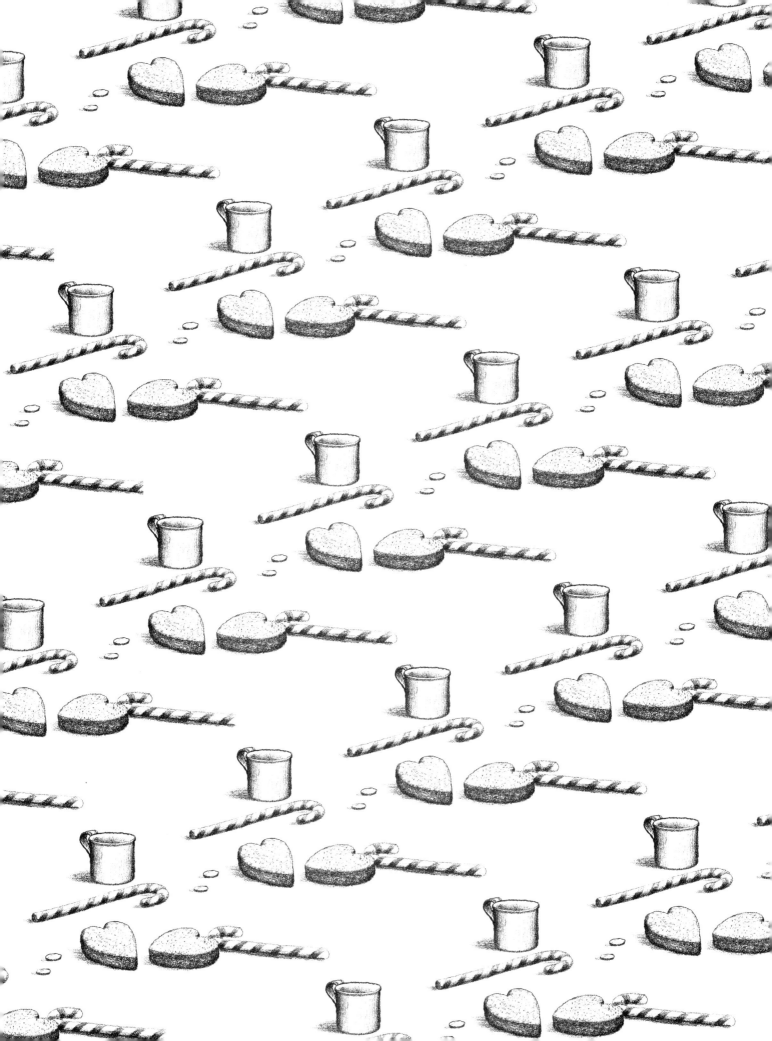